I SPY 123

Totally Crazy Numbers!

MANUELA ANCUTICI

ULRIKE SAUERHÖFER

FIREFLY BOOKS

AND THIS IS HOW IT WORKS

Welcome

There is something here for everyone to discover!

Follow the clues and solve the puzzles

by finding what is hidden inside each number.

In what number is the king of animals hiding?

Who can discover the 5 with eyes?

Where is the pig in a dress?

Have fun!

You will find the solution pages at the end of the book.

Q

Can you see what I can see?
There is an elephant with a big belly,
four tortoises, two horses
and a whole herd of cattle.

Look for a mother helping
with homework
and a parrot looking peaceful.
A sweet little butterfly that
flutters quietly back and forth.

Did you find the butterfly?
Can you see the brown monkey?
Can you find the coin from Egypt?
Finally, show me three tens!

Can you see what I can see?
Look for two tiny yellow boots and
two greenish-blue cowboy
boots hidden in this mess.

Wow, you think that was hard?
Try and find the two pink boots
and make sure that they're buckled.
You won't find them in a flash.

Now try and find, and this isn't a joke,
a white shoe with a heart
and two red ice skates.
You can find them all if you try!

Can you see what I can see?
There are three hidden soccer balls.
But it's much harder to find the
giraffe-patterned rubber ball.

Look for three hearts and a
ball that sticks out its tongue!
Spiderman's face is hiding here
and so is a cute green alien.

A ladybug and two orange bees.
Can you find all three?
There are three balls with the
number 3 on them for you to find.

Can you see what I can see?
A rabbit watering the garden,
a hanger for clothes, a tiny chair
and four ghosts with
arms stretched out.

A spotted puppy dog is missing.
Find him fast!
The number 3, a toy soldier with
black boots and Donald Duck are
well hidden, but can you find them?

Somewhere there is an elephant
that never forgets. Find the
beautiful fairy with wings, a
little yellow owl and a green car.

Can you see what I can see?
Find a little white ghost and
a helmet with a large gemstone.
I hope you see them too.

From the age of chivalry
there is a damsel, although
she is not in distress.
Two archers are with her.

Five dragons are still hidden here,
have you already discovered the key?
What is in the chest?
You'll find them all if you search carefully.

Can you see what I can see?
Find a Smurf with a very soft hat,
six pigs and a deer wearing a scarf
because of a sore throat.
The lion, king of all animals,
would like to catch the mice, all four.
Two frogs croak in a duet,
while three elephants play in a trio.

Two crows are still hidden here,
you'll find them, do not worry.
And the dragon with the hat?
When you find him you'll be done.

Can you see what I can see?
There are seven pairs of pants
and a headset hidden here.
Try and find them for yourself!

A pink sweater is missing.
Does it belong to a princess?
There is a crown on it too.
It makes it look more festive.

For cool guys who like chilling,
there are four sunglasses.
Do you like the Wild West?
Then look for the cowboy hat.

Can you see what I can see?
Find a red parrot, very well hidden.
Although you can hardly believe it,
there's even a 5 with eyes.

A siren blares, just listen,
here comes the fire truck.
Can you see the three golden
lions and the little fox?

Look for nine fish swimming.
Then find the eight knights,
proud as Sir Lancelot, with
armour silver and deep red.

Can you see what I can see?
Three shamrocks, do you see them?
Two caterpillars crawl away quickly,
but you're fast you'll catch them.

Two feathers float away, you'll
see them right away, it's not difficult.
There are four frogs that make
a very nice croaking quartet.

When they're not working,
three ants can be found here.
Finally, can you discover the
four snail shells on this page?

Can you see what I can see?
A knife from the table and three
scissors are hidden here.
Did you find the camera?

The fish surely came out of the sea,
the seahorse probably did the same.
A beautiful deer is hidden here too.
Did you find the little bunny?

Now find me some more things. First,
the numbers 2 and 7. Then two
walkie-talkies that are well hidden.
You also need to find the five keys.

Can you see what I can see?
Look for the two beautiful blue
hearts, three yellow monkeys that
screech and two quiet deer.

Please find a small violet heart,
eleven woolly sheep,
(only one is easy to see),
and a mushroom that is blue.

Now, look quickly for these things:
Six owls, fashionably styled.
Four purple horses and
four large elephants as well.

Can you see what I can see?
You will have to look closely!
Can you see two grandmas with gray hair?
Do you know where the eye patch is?

Do you see a cute pig?
The green dragon looks pretty happy.
Then show me the seven stars,
I like to look at the night sky.

Can you find the red hat with a bell?
The devil is making mischief.
Where is he, can you see him,
with his gold horns and red face?

HAPPY

Can you see what I can see?
This number has a birthday party
that looks like fun. Find the red eight
and then the frog. Well done!

A cute little pink pig comes
to the celebration in a dress.
A polar bear from the North Pole
with four owls looking festive.

A green P is hiding somewhere.
Did you find the baby chick?
Now look again because there's
a funny dolphin swimming here.

Can you see what I can see?
Seven burgers are well hidden.
Now we'll go on a scavenger hunt.
There's no telling what you'll find!

Five fried eggs, how nice and tasty
and two oranges must be found.
Two candy canes are needed and
two chilli peppers, devilishly hot.

Five green mice quickly disappear
so the two cats can not find them.
Then look carefully and you'll
see two worms and five tennis balls.

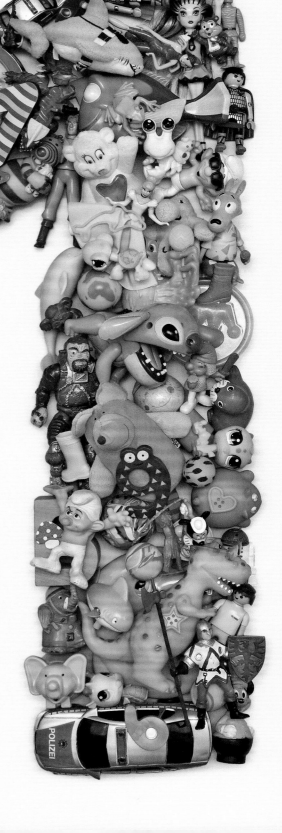

Q

Can you see what I can see?
There is a small seashell hidden
somewhere inside this number.
Find a dinosaur that wears glasses.

There is a knight with a sword for courage.
A cute bear has a heart on its stomach.
There are three pirates on board.
Look carefully and you'll find them all.

Two beautiful blue horses and
an old woman with gray hair,
plus two aliens with three eyes.
Superman completes your search!

Now it's time to play, be ready!
The hourglass stops for you.
Three wooden buttons in light brown,
you just have to look very carefully.

A dice with a red dot,
you can find it, just look.
And then you discover with good luck
pick-up sticks, look, ten pieces.

Pippi Longstocking is looking for her horse,
you must help her find him fast.
A cardboard disk with a white eight
you'll soon see. Well done!

Here, standing ready for you, are
a vegetable mix and fruit salad.
Five blueberries, thick and blue,
two almonds, look carefully.

The hazelnuts number three,
the pickles number five.
A gooseberry, all alone,
also still remains to be found.

Look further, it will be worth it.
There are four thin long beans.
My, the olives are small, but you
should find two green ones.

Can you see what I see?
Let's take a closer look:
a little bag should be here
and two small clean brushes.

The animals look so happy!
A bunny hears music with it's
long ears. There are six hippos and
two elephants from Africa.

Find these things they aren't
difficult, a sweet pink teddy bear,
a heart, two car beetles and finally
the magical horse Pegasus!

First, definitely find the beach ball
that the lady is holding.
Two hunters are still here and
there is a small dancing pig.

Where is it, where is it,
the beautiful old pocket watch?
The alligator and the teddy bear
are much easier to find.

Where is the king, where is he?
Is it his pocket watch?
An ice cream cart full of flavor is
there for you to discover.

Q

Now this last number is orange.
Search for the turtle with a hat.
Show me six tigers next
and then the two pigs.

Three airplanes and in the middle,
is a beautiful queen.
Eleven foxes hunt again while
the caterpillar crawls slowly.

A squeaky rubber duck is
here to end it all!
Searching is such hard work.
Be proud of what you've found!

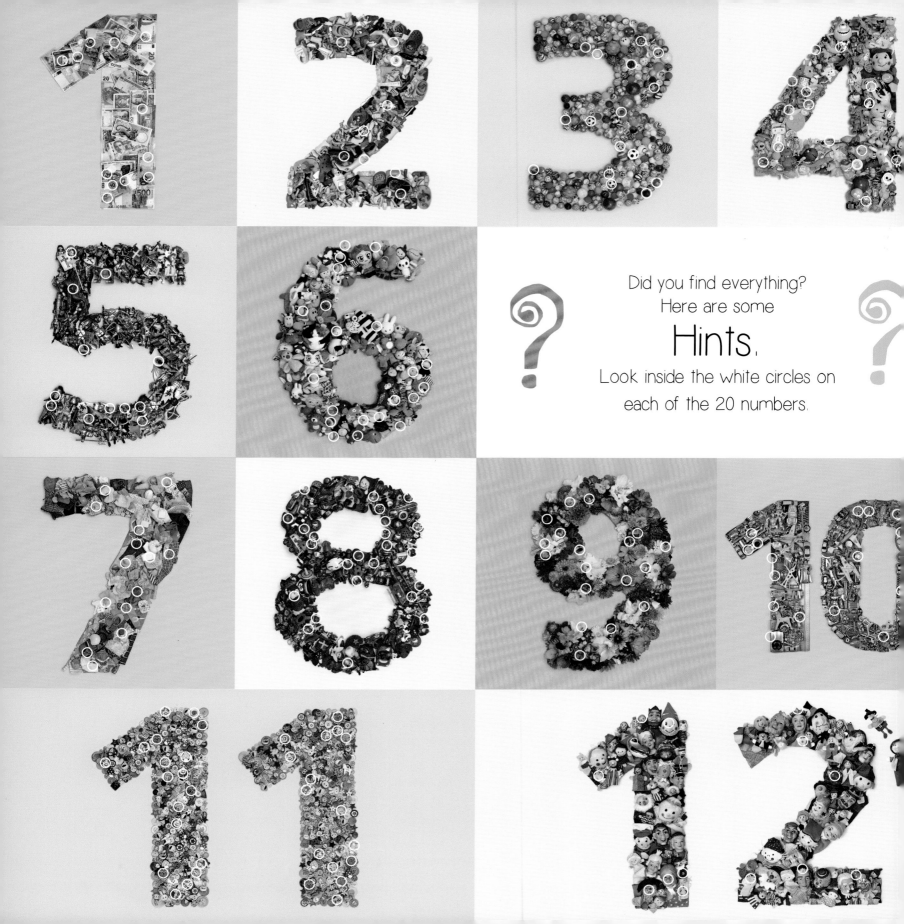

Did you find everything?
Here are some
Hints.
Look inside the white circles on
each of the 20 numbers.

A FIREFLY BOOK

Published by Firefly Books Ltd. 2017

First printing

Publisher Cataloging-in-Publication Data (U.S.)

Library of Congress Cataloging-in-Publication Data is available

Library and Archives Canada Cataloguing in Publication

Sauerhöfer, Ulrike
[Ich sehe was, was du nicht siehst, die total verrückten Zahlen. English]
  I spy 123 : totally crazy numbers! / Ulrike Sauerhöfer ; illustrated and designed by Manuela Ancutici.
Translation of: Ich sehe was, was du nicht siehst, die total verrückten Zahlen.
ISBN 978-1-77085-999-9 (hardcover)
  1. Picture puzzles — Juvenile literature. 2. Picture puzzles.
I. Ancutici, Manuela, illustrator II. Title. III. Title: I spy 1 2 3.
IV. Title: I spy one two three. V. Title: Ich sehe was, was du nicht siehst, die total verrückten Zahlen. English
GV1507.P47S2813 2017   j793.73   C2017-902100-1

Published in the United States by
Firefly Books (U.S.) Inc.
P.O. Box 1338, Ellicott Station
Buffalo, New York 14205

Published in Canada by
Firefly Books Ltd.
50 Staples Avenue, Unit 1
Richmond Hill, Ontario L4B 0A7

Translator: Michael Worek

Printed in China

Thanks to Susanne, Phine, Jessica, Philippe, Anne-Marie, Finya, Katharina, Julian, Connie, Agathe, Nicole, Heike, Linus, Jonas, Maya and Mila, who enriched the pictures with their toys and special objects.

Canada

We acknowledge the financial support of the Government of Canada.

Editor: Ruth Prenting
Original German text: Ulrike Sauerhöfer
Design and composition: Ancutici kommunikationsdesign
Production: Verena Schmynec